THE SECRET GARDEN

™

A novelization by M.J. Carr
Based on the screenplay by Caroline Thompson

SCHOLASTIC INC.
New York Toronto London Auckland Sydney

WARNER BROS. PRESENTS
AN AMERICAN ZOETROPE PRODUCTION A FILM BY AGNIESZKA HOLLAND
"THE SECRET GARDEN" KATE MABERLY HEYDON PROWSE
ANDREW KNOTT AND MAGGIE SMITH MUSIC BY ZBIGNIEW PREISNER
EXECUTIVE PRODUCER FRANCIS FORD COPPOLA SCREENPLAY BY CAROLINE THOMPSON
BASED ON THE BOOK BY FRANCES HODGSON BURNETT
PRODUCED BY FRED FUCHS, FRED ROOS AND TOM LUDDY
DIRECTED BY AGNIESZKA HOLLAND

WARNER BROS.
A TIME WARNER ENTERTAINMENT COMPANY

ISBN 0-590-47172-4

12 11 10 9 8 7 6 5 4 3 2   3 4 5 6 7 8/9

Printed in the U.S.A.   40

First Scholastic printing, May 1993

1

Mary Lennox was a sour little girl. Her skin was pale as powder and her frame as thin as a twig. The features of her face seemed always to be worked into a tight, irritable scowl.

Mary Lennox lived in India. Her father was a British general, and her mother was quite beautiful. Mary's parents didn't have a lot of time for her. Mary was cared for by an Indian woman, her Ayah, who each day dressed her in pretty dresses — though Mary was well past old enough to dress herself.

"Come away from there, Miss Mary!" the Ayah called one afternoon.

Mary was sitting outside her family's bungalow, beside a muddy, black pond. In her hand she held some flowers. They were wilted and nearly dead. Mary had sneaked them from the vases inside the house.

"Stand, pigs!" Mary commanded the flowers. She

tried to plant them in the earth, but the flowers had already been cut and had no roots. "Daughters of pigs!" Mary said angrily. It was the worst insult she could think of.

As Mary moved closer to the edge of the pond, she lost her balance and fell in. Mary ran, shrieking and muddy, back to the bungalow and into her mother's bedroom. Her Ayah followed close behind.

Mary's mother was sitting at her dressing table, getting ready for a grand party that was to be held in honor of the Maharajah. As she swept her hair up into a jeweled hair comb, she noticed her daughter in the reflection of her mirror.

"You've ruined your new dress," she said icily. "Ayah will put you into a warm bath before you catch cold."

"But I want to be with you at the party!" Mary protested. "I can wear another dress!"

"There isn't time," said her mother.

Ayah pulled Mary, kicking and screaming, from her mother's room. Mary's mother watched her and shook her head. "I haven't the strength for that child," she said.

That night, Mary stood in her nightgown, looking out the window at the lights of the party beyond. Servants holding torches ringed the compound. Elephants were tethered in the courtyard. Mary could hear an orchestra playing festive dance music.

Mary stomped angrily into her parents' room. On her mother's dressing table sat a miniature carved ivory elephant. Mary picked it up and hurled it against the wall. Its trunk broke off, sharp and jagged. Mary clutched the broken elephant in her hand and crawled under her parents' bed. It was her own private place.

Just as she settled herself, however, a rumble sounded. The bed above Mary began to shake, as did the floor of the room, and the walls. Mary clutched the elephant tighter. She heard people screaming and wailing.

"Earthquake!" someone shouted. "Help!"

Suddenly, the walls of the room buckled. The ceiling of the bungalow caved down around the bed.

After that, all was quiet in the dark, black night.

2

The next morning, the bright Indian sun poked through the crevices of the debris. Under the bed, Mary opened her eyes. A thin stream of blood trickled down her forehead. Around her, Mary heard footsteps. She tried to cry out, but she was too weak.

Suddenly a large, snakelike creature poked its way through the debris and sniffed at her face. Then it wrapped itself around one of the broken legs of the bed and lifted the bed high. It wasn't a snake, it was the trunk of an elephant! Rescue workers gasped to see the pale girl huddled underneath the bed.

"A child!" said one. "I didn't know there was a child!"

The workers lifted Mary onto a litter and carried her out of the wreckage of the bungalow. Mary clutched the ivory elephant from her mother's dressing table. Mary was alive. But she would soon find out that her parents — and all those at the party — had died in the terrible earthquake.

Because there was no longer anyone to care for her, Mary had to travel back to England. The authorities put her on a ship along with all the other English children who had been orphaned by the earthquake.

Mary was more nasty-tempered now than ever. Though the journey was long, she did not make friends with any of the other children. They taunted her. "Mistress Mary, quite contrary," one chanted. The others joined in:

> *"Mistress Mary, quite contrary,*
> *How does your garden grow?*
> *With silver bells, and cockleshells,*
> *And pretty maids all in a row."*

When the boat arrived in England, the children ran down the gangplank and crowded on the dock, waiting for their relatives to claim them. It was an emotional scene. Aunts and uncles, cousins and grandparents rushed up to hug the orphans and bring them home. No one was there, though, to meet Mary.

"Mary Lennox?" said a voice.

Mary looked up. Above her stood a woman. The

woman was wearing a black dress, a black bonnet, and a black shawl.

"I'm Mrs. Medlock," said the woman. "I'm the housekeeper for Misselthwaite Manor. Your uncle, Archibald Craven, sent me to get you."

Mary stood stock-still. She pursed her lips tightly.

Mrs. Medlock looked Mary up and down. "What a queer, unresponsive little thing," she said. "And, my word! A plain piece of goods, too! We'd heard your mother was a beauty. She certainly didn't hand much of it down, did she?"

Mrs. Medlock lifted Mary into a carriage. The two traveled all night across the wet, rainy countryside to get to Misselthwaite Manor. Mary sat stiffly, her hands folded in her lap. She stared out the window of the carriage as Mrs. Medlock prattled on.

"Your uncle's not going to trouble himself about you, that's sure and certain," she said. "He never troubles himself about no one. He's got a crooked back. And if that weren't cross enough for a man to bear, then *she* had to up and die."

Mary looked at Mrs. Medlock quizzically.

"Yes, that's right," Mrs. Medlock said. "Your aunt is dead. Didn't your mother tell you?"

"My mother didn't have time to tell me stories," Mary said curtly.

Mrs. Medlock pulled a sandwich out of a hamper

and offered it to Mary. Mary turned away without taking it and looked back out the window. The dreary moor stretched ahead as far as she could see.

As dawn broke, the carriage pulled up to the entrance of a large estate. By the gate of the estate, there was a small cottage. A red-cheeked boy darted out of the cottage and opened the gate to let the carriage through.

"We're here," said Mrs. Medlock.

Ahead of the carriage, Mary saw a large, lonely-looking house.

"There's Misselthwaite now," Mrs. Medlock told her.

Mary had arrived at her new home.

3

When Mary woke up the next morning, she was in a large bed in a large room. She felt lost and little. Footsteps echoed in the hallway outside her room. It was Mrs. Medlock. She had a tray in her hands.

"Here's your breakfast," she said gruffly. "Get up."

"Who's going to dress me?" asked Mary.

Mrs. Medlock stared at her in disbelief. "You can't dress yourself?" she asked.

"Of course not," said Mary. "My Ayah dressed me."

"As old as you are!" Mrs. Medlock shook her head. "What do they do to children over there, carry you around in a basket?"

Mary was not used to being spoken to this way by servants. She stood up imperiously on her bed.

"How dare you talk to me with disrespect!" she said.

Mrs. Medlock snorted. "You're going to have to look after yourself here," she said. "And you needn't expect to see your uncle, because it's certain you won't. There are near a hundred rooms in this house," she went on. "This one and no other is yours. You're not to touch anything and you're not to go wandering and poking about."

A hundred rooms! Mary nodded sullenly.

When Mrs. Medlock left, Mary took her ivory elephant out from under her pillow. She turned up her nose at the bowl of porridge that Mrs. Medlock had brought her for breakfast. She looked outside the window at the cold, lonely moor.

The wind was howling and moaning. Suddenly, Mary heard another cry. This one sounded like it came from a person. Mary ran to her doorway. The cry was fainter. It seemed to come from somewhere on the other side of the wall of her room.

In one corner of the wall, Mary spotted a tiny door. The door was way too short for an adult. Though Mary was still in her nightgown, she dropped to her knees and crawled through.

On the other side of the door was an old hallway. The walls were crumbling. At the end of the hallway Mary spotted another tiny door. When she crawled through, she found herself in a strange, wild room.

The room was overgrown with vines that had crept in from a crack in the window. At one end of the room was a dressing table. On it was a carved ivory elephant just like her mother's! Next to the elephant was a photograph. In it, two women were sitting on a swing in a beautiful garden. One of the women was her mother. And the other woman looked almost exactly like her. They were clearly twins.

"It must be my aunt," thought Mary. "This must have been my aunt's room."

As Mary set down the photograph, she heard a tinkly, musical sound. It seemed to come from inside the dressing table. Mary opened the drawer. Inside was a music box. Inside the music box was an old-fashioned key. The top of the key was etched with a beautiful design.

This certainly was a mysterious house. Mary wanted to explore more rooms. She wandered into the hallway. Down the hall was a grand staircase. As Mary drew near, she heard the crying again. It was coming from the top of the stairs. Mary started up. The crying got louder.

At the top of the stairs and down a long hallway was a large, dusty tapestry. Mary pulled it aside. It was hiding another long hallway. There was a person in the hallway walking toward her. It was Mrs. Medlock!

"What are you doing?" Mrs. Medlock cried angrily. "I thought I told you to stay in your room!"

"I heard someone crying," said Mary.

"The dogs," Mrs. Medlock answered. "Your uncle keeps dogs."

"No," Mary protested. "It was a person crying."

"You heard nothing of the sort," snapped Mrs. Medlock.

Mrs. Medlock grabbed Mary's arm and yanked her down the hallway, through the maze of more hallways, and back to Mary's own room.

"You stay here," she said. "Or I'll box your ears!"

Mrs. Medlock shoved Mary into the bedroom. Mary stared at her, dumbfounded. The door slammed in her face.

It seemed to Mary that there were many secrets in this house.

4

There was not a lot for Mary to do, locked in her room. It seemed she was stuck there forever. No one came to talk to her, or even to dress her. Her only friend was the little ivory elephant.

As morning turned to afternoon, Mary again heard footsteps in the hallway. This time, a young housemaid came in. Her name was Martha. She was carrying Mary's lunch on a tray.

"Good afternoon," said Martha cheerfully. She had a strange lilt to her speech. It was hard for Mary to understand what she was saying.

Martha set the lunch tray down on Mary's table, next to the breakfast tray. "Here," she said. She looked surprised. "You never touched your breakfast. You didn't want your porridge?"

"No," said Mary.

"Tha' doesn't know how good it is," said Martha.

"You should put a bit o' treacle on it, or some sugar."

"I didn't want it," Mary insisted sourly.

"Eh!" said Martha. "There's twelve of us at home. If any of my little brothers or sisters was at this table, they'd clean it bare in five minutes!"

"Why?" asked Mary.

"Why!" cried Martha. Now she looked even more surprised. "Because in this world you take a full stomach when you can get one."

"I don't know what it is to be hungry," sniffed Mary. "Are you my servant?"

"I do the housemaid's work," explained Martha. "I'll be waiting on you a bit."

That was enough of an answer for Mary. She marched over to the wardrobe and held out her arms, waiting to be dressed. Martha looked at Mary's outstretched arms. She reached under and gave Mary a little tickle.

"Stop it!" cried Mary, indignantly. "What are you doing?"

"I thought all girls liked to be tickled," said Martha, smiling playfully.

"I won't be laughed at, servant!" Mary shouted. She stomped her feet and kicked and screamed. Martha had never seen such a tantrum.

"Please, don't be vexed," said Martha. Her voice was calm and soothing. "I beg your pardon, Miss."

Martha selected a dress from Mary's wardrobe and slipped it over her head. She reached around to button Mary up.

"I don't know when exactly your uncle will call for you," Martha said.

"My uncle?" Mary interrupted. "Mrs. Medlock said he wouldn't want to see me."

"Ah, but he does," said Martha, smiling.

Mary sat down and lifted up her feet so that Martha could put her shoes and stockings on her. When Martha had Mary dressed properly, she left her alone again in the room.

Mary sat stiffly in her chair, waiting. She folded her hands in her lap. She wondered how long it would be until she'd be called to meet her uncle.

But the afternoon passed, as had the morning. The day grew dark. Still, no one came for Mary. When the sun began to set, Mrs. Medlock appeared at Mary's door.

"His Lordship has decided not to see you today," she said. That was all.

"But when will I see him?" Mary asked. "Tomorrow?"

Mrs. Medlock shook her head. "He'll be gone tomorrow," she said.

Mrs. Medlock closed the door.

That night, late, Mary lay in her bed, unable to sleep. She heard someone coming down the hall, someone with heavy footsteps. Mary's door creaked open. A wedge of light streamed through. Mary saw a dark figure, a man. He had hunched shoulders and carried a candle in his hand.

Mary squeezed her eyes shut, pretending to be asleep. The man walked over to Mary's bed. Though Mary's eyes were closed, she knew that the man was staring at her. After awhile, the man left.

Later that night, just before dawn, Mary heard a sound outside the window. In the courtyard was a man, the one who had come to her room. Now he was wearing a great, black traveling cape.

Mary watched as the man climbed into a carriage. When the driver of the carriage cracked his whip, the horses started up. Mary watched the carriage as it drove off. Soon it was hidden by the thick fog that blanketed the moor.

"That must have been my uncle," thought Mary.

The moonlight lit her pale, thin face.

Things in this household were getting stranger and stranger.

5

The next day, Mary was glad that it was Martha who brought her breakfast to her. When Mary had eaten, Martha dressed her. She dressed her warmly, in sweaters and scarves. Martha was dressing Mary to go outside.

"But I have nothing to play with," said Mary.

"Nothing to play with!" said Martha. She'd never heard of such a thing. "What about the sticks and the stones? My brother Dickon plays on th' moor by himself for hours."

"Who?" asked Mary.

"Dickon," said Martha. "My younger brother. That's how he made friends with the pony."

Martha buttoned Mary's coat.

"There," she said. "Tha's ready to go out now." She clapped a cap on Mary's head and led her to the kitchen door.

Outside, the cold wind gusted. Martha pointed to a gate.

"To get to the gardens you must go through there," she said.

She gave Mary a little push outside.

"Run along now," she said. "Have fun!"

Mary stumbled out the door and looked around at the vast estate. She trundled off toward the gardens.

As Mary passed a hedge of bushes, she felt that someone was watching her. Someone was. It was a young boy, hiding behind the hedge. Beside him was a little red fox. The little fox stuck his snout through a hole in the bushes and sniffed at Mary. Mary whipped around, but she couldn't see anyone. The boy and the fox were hidden well.

All of the gardens on the estate were planted inside high stone walls. Mary found the door to the first garden easily enough. The door was open, so Mary went inside.

Because it was winter, the garden was bare and scraggly. Mary passed through that garden and into the door to the next. Each of the gardens led to another. Finally, Mary came to a tall stone wall covered thickly with vines.

A robin perched on top of the wall looked down at Mary. He cocked his head and chirped. He seemed to be trying to tell her something. High in the wall, there was a small window. Mary stood on her toes to peer through. On the other side of the wall was yet another garden. But there didn't seem to be any door leading to this one. Mary felt her way along the wall, searching for the door.

"You there!" Mary called. She had spotted a gardener pushing a wheelbarrow into another garden. "Where's the door to that garden?" she demanded. "I didn't see a door."

"It's shut up," mumbled the gardener. He was an old man with a weathered face.

"But where's the door?" Mary persisted.

The gardener began digging in one of the flower beds.

"No one's been inside that place for ten years," he said. "The dead are dead and gone and better off left that way."

"Who's dead?" Mary asked.

The gardener didn't answer.

"My aunt's dead," Mary said thoughtfully. She considered this a moment. "It was *her* garden, wasn't it?"

The gardener kept at his work.

"It's revolting the way you people behave toward me!" said Mary. She couldn't stand to be ignored. "Tell me your name so I can report you!"

"Ben Weatherstaff," said the gardener. "You certainly are disagreeable."

Just then the robin flew near them and burst into song. Ben Weatherstaff laughed.

"I don't know why," he said, "but it looks as if he's decided to make friends with you."

"He has?" Mary asked. "I've never had any friends," she admitted.

Just then, the robin flew off, toward the locked garden. Mary chased after him, leaving Ben Weatherstaff to his work. The robin landed on the garden wall and sang brightly.

Mary grabbed ahold of the stones in the wall and tried to hoist herself up and over. Before she reached the top, she slipped and fell back. Someone behind her laughed. It was a boy's laugh.

"Who's there?" Mary demanded. The boy laughed again. It was coming from another of the gardens. Mary ran into the garden. She saw the boy. Beside him was the little red fox. The boy ran in one direction and the fox ran in another.

Mary chased after the boy, but he ran faster. He raced through a large gate that led to the moor. He hopped on a pony that was grazing there and galloped away.

"Who are you?" Mary called after him.

Mary didn't know it, but the boy was Martha's brother. The boy she had seen was Dickon.

6

Every morning that week, Martha dressed Mary warmly and sent her out to the gardens to play. One morning, Mary asked Martha about the secret, locked garden.

"Why does Lord Craven want my aunt's garden kept locked?" asked Mary. "Why does he hate her garden?"

"We're not supposed to talk about it," Martha whispered. She handed Mary a skipping rope and shooed her outside.

Mary skipped into the gardens. She liked the feeling of skipping rope. She had never done it before. She skipped past Ben Weatherstaff. Suddenly, she heard chirping. Mary looked up. Above her was a robin.

"Is that you?" Mary asked the robin.

The robin trilled a pretty song and started to fly off. He seemed to be beckoning Mary to follow.

The robin flew directly to the vine-covered wall of the secret garden.

"It *is* you!" cried Mary.

The robin pecked at a patch of ivy. It seemed to Mary as if he were trying to show her something. Mary tugged at the patch of ivy, tearing it from the wall. Behind the ivy was a door! The door to the secret garden! Mary tried to turn the knob, but it was locked.

Then Mary noticed the brass plate over the keyhole. It was etched with a beautiful scroll. Mary knew she had seen that sort of scroll work before. The key! The key she had found in her aunt's dressing room! The day she had come upon the wild room that was overgrown with vines!

Mary hurried back to the house. She slipped in quietly so none of the servants would see her and made her way to the overgrown room. The key was just where she'd left it.

As Mary pocketed the key, she heard a crying sound. It was the same, queer sound she had heard before. The crying grew louder. Mary ducked back into the room as Mrs. Medlock bustled down the hall, headed for the cries.

Mary was curious about the cries, but she had another secret to attend to — the garden. With the key in her pocket, Mary ran back and tried the key in the garden door. The key turned! Mary pushed at the door. It was swollen and weathered. Mary pushed harder. The door creaked open!

Inside the door was a garden that was much bigger than the others. It was overgrown, and much of it seemed dead. Still, it was strikingly beautiful.

At the foot of a stone stairway was a little pond. Next to the pond were the ruins of an old church. Stone benches lined the walls. Tall flower urns proudly graced the paths. Mary stubbed her toe. There was something under the leaves. Mary kicked at the leaves and dug it out. It was an old camera mounted on a tripod stand.

"What a strange, beautiful place this is," thought Mary.

All around the garden were rosebushes. Mary ran her finger over the stems. They were brown and brittle. Maybe everything in the garden was dead.

Then Mary noticed a pale green point poking out of the damp soil. She knelt down to look closely. It was a new shoot of a plant. It wasn't dead at all.

Mary clawed at the earth around the little spike, clearing the area of leaves and weeds. She knew that if the little plant were to live, it would need room to grow. Mary didn't know how she knew this. No one had ever told her. But she knew.

Mary sat back on her heels and surveyed the garden around her. Slowly, she began to smile. It was the first time she had smiled since she came to

Misselthwaite Manor. It was, perhaps, the first time she had smiled in many years.

"Mary!" someone called. It was Martha's voice, calling from the house. "Ma-a-a-a-ary!"

Mary jumped up and bolted up the stone stairway. As she slipped out of the garden, an odd gust of wind stirred up the leaves where she had been sitting. The leaves swirled and swirled, as if they were taking shape.

Mary didn't notice, though. She closed the door behind her and locked it carefully, covering it again with vines.

Inside the locked garden, the leaves swirled into the shape of a beautiful spirit. It was Mary's Aunt Lilias. Though she had died, her presence remained in the garden she had loved.

The spirit floated past the pond and over the flower beds. Aunt Lilias had not yet left Misselthwaite Manor because she still had work to do. There were still some matters that needed her love and care.

7

The next morning, at breakfast, Martha was surprised to see Mary gobble up her porridge. The fresh air was giving Mary a healthy appetite. She even seemed to be getting a little pink in her cheeks.

Outside the window, the wind wailed. Another cry sounded above the wind. Mary had heard that cry before.

"Listen," she said. "Hear that?"

"It's the wind," Martha said quickly.

Mary looked at Martha skeptically. The cry sounded again. There was no mistaking. It was human.

"Poor little Betty Butterworth," Martha hurried on. "The scullery maid. She's had a toothache all morning."

Just then, Mrs. Medlock burst into Mary's room, clapping her hands. "Out!" she cried. "Martha, get the child out of doors at once!"

Martha hustled Mary into her coat. Clearly, there was something that Martha and Mrs. Medlock didn't want Mary to know.

Mary scuffed along the paths outside. She wondered who it was that was crying. Suddenly, a big crow swooped down and flew straight at her. Mary ducked.

A boy ran up. It was the same boy Mary had seen before. The crow swooped down and landed on his shoulder. Mary guessed that the boy was Dickon. Mary was right.

"Come," said Dickon. "His name's Soot. He won't hurt you."

Dickon started to pet the crow.

"He'll bite me," said Mary. "He's dirty."

"No," said Dickon. "He's soft. You'll like it."

Dickon took Mary's hand to help her. Just then, the robin landed on a branch nearby and began to sing. Dickon looked up, and whistled back. He knew how to whistle the same tune as the robin!

"The robin says he's glad to see you," said Dickon.

"How do you know?" said Mary hotly. "People can't talk to animals."

"They trust me," said Dickon. "They tell me their secrets."

"He didn't tell you *my* secret, did he?" asked

Mary quickly. "I don't know what I'd do if anybody found out about it."

"About what?" asked Dickon.

Mary didn't know whether to tell Dickon or not. But Dickon seemed so nice. And gentle . . .

"A garden," she blurted out. "I've stolen a garden. Maybe it's dead anyhow. I don't know."

"I'd know," offered Dickon.

"You would?" asked Mary. Her eyes widened. Here was someone who could help.

Mary led Dickon to the door of the secret garden. She unlocked the door and let them both inside. Dickon looked around at the tangle of weeds that cluttered the garden. He noticed the little green shoot poking out of the soil. He noticed that, all around it, the soil had been cleared.

"Who did this?" he asked.

"I did," said Mary. "It looked like it was strangling."

"It'll be a lily," said Dickon, nodding. "Maybe it's an Empress of India lily."

"Really?" Mary asked. She repeated the name out loud. It reminded her of her home.

Dickon took out his penknife and cut a stalk off of one of the rosebushes nearby.

"This garden's not dead at all," he said. "The old wood just needs to be cut away." He pointed to a stalk that was a little greener. "This part is wick," he said. "See the green?"

"Wick?" asked Mary. "What's wick?"

"Alive," Dickon explained. "Full of life. There'll be plenty of roses in here this summer."

Mary looked around, excited. Her eye fell on something she hadn't seen before. It was a wooden garden swing. It was the same swing she had seen in the photograph, the one on her Aunt Lilias's dressing table.

Dickon saw the swing as well.

"They say that's how she died," he said solemnly. "By falling off the swing."

"Really?" said Mary. She ran her hand over the rough wood of the swing.

That night, as Martha dressed Mary for bed, Mary told Martha that she'd met Dickon.

"Did you?" said Martha. "What do you think of him?"

"I think he's beautiful," gushed Mary.

Martha looked at Mary. Mary's eyes were lit up and sparkling. Martha had to laugh.

8

That night, Mary had a dream. In her dream was a beautiful woman. The woman looked like Mary's mother. Or her Aunt Lilias. The woman was hugging a child. But suddenly, the mother disappeared. The child started crying. Loud cries. Terrible cries.

Mary woke up from the dream. But the cries were not just in her dream, they were real. Mary lit the candle by her bed and listened outside her doorway. The cries grew louder.

Mary padded into the hallway. She followed the dark, winding hall toward the cries. Soon she came to a staircase she recognized. At the top of the staircase was the hallway with the heavy tapestry she had passed through before. Mary pressed on and pushed past the tapestry. At the end of the passageway she could see a bit of light. It was poking out from under a door. The cries were coming from the room just beyond.

When Mary opened the door, she saw a small, thin boy lying in a very large bed. The boy gasped. He stopped crying at the sight of her.

"Are you a ghost?" he whispered.

"No," croaked Mary. "Are you?"

"My name is Colin Craven," said the boy. "I'm the master of this house while my father's away."

Mary looked at him. "Then you're my cousin," she said. "Our mothers were sisters. Twins."

"Really?" said the boy. "Come here."

Mary walked closer to the bed. The boy was pale, paler than she had been when she arrived. His features were sharp and thin.

"Why were you crying?" asked Mary.

"I can't sleep," said Colin. He fidgeted irritably. "Plump my pillows," he demanded.

"What?" cried Mary. No one had ever before asked her to do servant's work. "I'll get Martha or Mrs. Medlock," she said.

"No!" cried Colin. "Medlock wouldn't allow you in here. She'd be afraid that you'd upset me and make me more ill."

Colin and Mary stared at each other across the dimly lit room.

"See that curtain?" asked Colin. A silk curtain

hung over the mantle near his bed. "Open it."

Mary pulled the cord to the curtain. Underneath the curtain was a large painting of Colin's mother. She looked exactly like Mary's mother. Mary stared and stared at it.

"Why do you keep a curtain over her?" Mary asked.

"Sometimes I hate her," said Colin. "She died when I was born."

"But I thought she died in her garden," said Mary. She didn't think before she said this. It just slipped out.

"Her garden?" asked Colin. "What garden?"

"Just a garden," Mary said quickly. "There are so many of them."

"Are there?" asked Colin.

"Of course," said Mary. "Don't you ever go outside?"

"Never," said Colin flatly. "I stay in this bed. I'm going to die."

Mary looked around the room. In the far corner she saw a wheelchair.

"You don't know how to walk?" she asked.

Colin shook his head no. "Will you come visit me every day?" he asked. "Though I don't know what Medlock would do if she found out."

"We won't tell her," said Mary. "It'll be another secret."

"Another secret?" asked Colin. "Are there more?"

Mary was finding it harder and harder to keep the secret of her garden.

"Your portrait's a kind of secret," she said, to cover up her mistake. "Then you were a secret from me. And I was a secret from you . . ."

"But not anymore," proclaimed Colin. "We're the ones with secrets now!"

Mary bit her lip. There were so many secrets to keep now, more than Colin could know.

9

The next morning, Mary was awake and out of bed at dawn. She ran to the window. The sky was still pink from the rising sun. The moor looked dewy and fresh.

Mary ran to her closet and pulled out a warm woolen dress. She wriggled it over her head and slipped her arms through the sleeves. Then she tried to button it up. The buttons were tiny, and her fingers were clumsy. Mary had never actually buttoned herself up before. But she kept doggedly at the task until she finished it.

Then there was the matter of her shoes. Mary jammed her left foot into her right shoe and her right foot into the left.

"Hmm," she said.

She switched the shoes, laced them up hurriedly, and chased off to the kitchen.

In the kitchen, all the servants were gathered

around the table, sipping their morning tea. They looked surprised to see Mary up and about so early.

"You dressed yourself!" exclaimed Martha.

Mary grinned. She grabbed her coat off the hook by the door, then raced outside.

By the time Mary reached the garden door, she was out of breath and panting. Dickon was leaning against the door, waiting for her.

"It's so early and you're already here!" said Mary.

"I've been waiting for hours," teased Dickon.

Mary pulled the key out of her pocket and once again unlocked the door to the secret garden.

Inside the garden, the two children knelt down by the first flower bed. The Empress of India lily had grown taller and stronger. That morning, Dickon had brought some gardening tools with him, and also a bag of seeds and bulbs. He showed Mary how to dig holes in the earth to plant the bulbs. They dug a ring of holes around the lily.

"We'll plant them all around your Empress of India," said Dickon.

"She'll have her own ladies-in-waiting," agreed Mary.

"Like in the rhyme," said Dickon. He started to sing:

> *"Mistress Mary, quite contrary,*
> *How does your garden grow?"*

Mary wasn't sure whether she should feel angry. That was the song that the other children on the boat had chanted to tease her. But the way Dickon was singing it was friendly. And besides, Mary thought, she *did* have a garden now. Mary joined in singing the rest of the song.

"With silver bells, and cockleshells,
And pretty maids all in a row."

"Are there really flowers called silver bells?" asked Mary.

Dickon nodded. "Cockleshells, too," he said.

"On the boat coming here they used to sing that song at me," she told Dickon. Mary frowned, thinking of how unhappy she had been. "I wasn't as contrary as they were." Mary wanted to change the subject. "I met my cousin last night," she said.

"You've seen Colin?" Dickon asked, surprised.

"You know about him?" asked Mary.

"Everybody knows about him, but hardly anybody's seen him."

"He said his mother died when he was born," said Mary.

"From falling off the swing," Dickon explained. "She fell off the swing and went into labor. He was born early."

Mary looked at her rosy-cheeked friend. "He's

34

not at all like you," she said. "His cheeks are whiter than ice and marble." She picked up one of the bulbs they were planting. "Whiter than these little hairs," she said, fingering the bulb.

"Those are the roots," explained Dickon. "Go on," he said. He pointed to the hole she had just dug. "Set it in there," he prodded.

Mary dropped the bulb in the hole. It fell in sideways. Dickon put his hand on Mary's and showed her how to right the bulb.

"Let it grow this way, Miss Mary," he said.

Together, the two children heaped some of the loose dirt back to cover the bulb. Together, they patted it down.

Together, Mary and Dickon were growing a garden.

10

When Mary finished planting, she sneaked back into the house and up to Colin's room. Colin's room was dark, as it always was. Heavy wooden shutters covered the windows. Mary tugged at the shutters to let in some air and light. The shutters wouldn't budge.

"Get away from there!" cried Colin. "They're nailed shut! My lungs can't take the spores!"

"Spores?" Mary asked. She had no idea what Colin was talking about.

"Spores are carried in on the wind," Colin said. He picked nervously at his nightclothes. "When you breathe the air, you swallow them. They stick in your lungs."

Mary didn't think that sounded right. Fresh air was healthy. Especially the clean, fresh air off the moor.

"Before I got out into the wind," she said, "even my hair was scrawny."

"But I'm going to die soon," he said. "I'll get a hump on my back like my father."

Mary made a face. "I hate the way you talk about dying," she said.

"Everybody thinks I'll die," said Colin.

"If everybody thought I was going to die," said Mary, as contrary as ever, "I wouldn't do it."

Colin reached into a drawer next to his bed. He pulled out a cloth face mask, the kind people wear in hospitals and sick rooms.

"Put this on," he demanded. "Everyone has to wear one. Medlock's orders."

Mary fitted the mask over her face. "It makes my face itch," she complained. She tore it off. "I didn't give you any germs last night, did I?"

"Put it on!" Colin commanded.

"Stop talking to me as if you were a Rajah," she shot back. "With emeralds and diamonds and rubies stuck all over you!"

Mary started to march toward the door.

"Where are you going?" Colin called after her.

"Back outside to be with Dickon," Mary threatened. "He tames animals like the animal charmers in India. And he knows everything there is to know about gardens."

"Does he know about my mother's garden?" asked Colin.

"What?" asked Mary. She wheeled around. How did Colin know about the garden?

"You told me my mother had a garden," he said.

"But how would Dickon know about it?" said Mary, trying to protect her secret. "It's locked. Nobody's allowed in."

"Well," said Colin imperiously. "I could make them unlock it."

"No!" cried Mary. "Don't do that! If you make them open the door, it wouldn't be a secret anymore!"

Colin looked unsure.

"Maybe you don't know how to keep a secret," Mary challenged him.

Colin didn't have time to answer. For, just then, a key jangled in the lock of his door.

"Medlock!" Colin whispered.

Mary looked around frantically for somewhere to hide. She dove under the bed. The door opened. In walked Mrs. Medlock and Martha. They had come to give Colin a treatment for his legs.

Mrs. Medlock set her medical bag at the foot of Colin's bed.

"Your father returns today," she told him.

"He won't want to see me," said Colin, as if he didn't care.

Mrs. Medlock arranged Colin's bed. Martha glanced down and saw Mary's foot sticking out from under the bed. She tapped it with her toe. Mary pulled her foot back under.

"Oh, dear," worried Mrs. Medlock. "I've forgotten my herbs."

She bustled out of the room to fetch what she'd forgotten. When she was gone, Martha stooped down and peered under the bed.

"What are you doing down there, Miss Mary?" she wailed. "If Mrs. Medlock finds out . . . oh, the world's comin' to an end!"

"She'll never let you come back here," Colin said to Mary. He was afraid of Mrs. Medlock, too.

"Go!" they both urged her. "Go!"

As Mary hurried back to her room, she heard dogs barking. The servants were calling to each other excitedly. "He's back!" they cried. "To your posts!"

Lord Craven had returned. Maybe Mary would meet her uncle at last.

11

Mary waited in her room all that afternoon, but her uncle did not call for her. That night, she couldn't sleep. She wandered through the halls to Colin's room. Colin was in his bed, asleep, but Mary did not go in. Lord Craven was standing over the boy's bed. He was watching Colin, just as he had watched Mary. His eyes looked lonely and sorrowful.

Mary crept back to her room. Her uncle was a strange man. If he wanted to see the children, why didn't he visit them in the daytime?

The next morning, when Mary awoke, Martha came and dressed her in her best dress. Then she took Mary's hand and led her to the library. Lord Craven had finally called.

Mary trembled as she stood in the doorway. Her uncle sat slumped in front of the fire.

"Come here!" he commanded.

Mary stood frozen in place. Her feet wouldn't move. She was scared. Slowly, she walked to his chair. As she drew near, Lord Craven drew a sharp breath.

"Your eyes. They look so much like . . ." Lord Craven stared at Mary's face. He went to his writing table and rummaged through a pile of papers.

"They never sent me your picture," he said, as if that explained something.

Lord Craven pulled a photograph of someone out of the pile. He stared at it a long time. It was as if he had forgotten that Mary was there. Finally, he turned around.

"Medlock wants me to send you to some sort of boarding school," he said.

"No!" cried Mary. "Please let me stay. I don't do any harm."

Lord Craven laughed a cold, bitter laugh. "Harm? What harm could you do? But there's nothing for a child here."

"I don't need much," Mary pleaded.

Lord Craven turned and poked at the fire. Mary wanted to ask her uncle something. Something important. She knew that if she didn't ask him now, she might never get the chance.

"All I need is — " she started to say. She choked back the lump in her throat and screwed up her courage. "Could I have a bit of earth?" she asked.

"A bit of earth?" Lord Craven knit his brow.

"To plant seeds in," Mary explained. "To make things grow."

Lord Craven laughed out loud. "Take your bit of earth," he said. "But don't be foolish enough to expect anything to come of it."

Mary knew there was more she needed to ask. "May I take it from anywhere?" she went on. "As long as it's not wanted?"

"Anywhere," Lord Craven barked. He wanted the visit done with. He turned back to the fire. "I'll be away till autumn," he said abruptly. "Now go!"

Mary scooted out the door. Her heart was soaring. Lord Craven had said she could have a bit of earth! That meant he gave her permission to tend the secret garden! He had said she could take the land from anywhere, hadn't he? As long as it was a place that wasn't wanted? Mary knew for certain that Lord Craven didn't want the secret garden. After all, he'd ordered it locked.

Mary tore toward the kitchen and grabbed her coat. She raced for the garden. As she rounded a corner, she spotted Dickon. He was playing a bright, airy tune on a crudely carved pipe.

Dickon's friends, the animals, were clustered around him. As Mary ran toward them, the animals scattered. All except the robin. The robin tilted his head and chirped, as if to say hello.

"Your robin sure likes you," said Dickon.

"That's one friend for me then," said Mary. She broke into a wide grin.

"Two," Dickon corrected her. He smiled shyly.

"Two?" asked Mary. She didn't understand. "Who else?"

Before Dickon could answer, he was interrupted by a clattering sound. It was the carriage, rumbling down the drive.

Mary and Dickon ran toward the drive in time to see that Lord Craven was in the carriage. He was leaving as quickly as he'd arrived. The two stared as the carriage rattled down the drive and out the gate. It began to rain.

"The rain's good for the flowers," Dickon said softly.

Mary wished, somehow, that her uncle had wanted to stay.

12

The rains that started when Lord Craven left did not stop. That night, as Mary visited Colin, rain pelted the shuttered windows.

"In India," said Mary, "when it rained, my Ayah would tell me stories." It seemed a long time since Mary had been in India.

"Stories?" said Colin. "About what?"

"The gods and goddesses, mostly," said Mary. "One of the gods was very powerful. When you looked down his throat, you could see the whole universe there."

"That's stupid," said Colin. "It doesn't make any sense."

Mary was tired of Colin's haughtiness. "It isn't stupid," she said hotly. "It's magic. You don't even want to understand!"

Mary jumped off the bed and headed for the door.

"You can't leave," said Colin. "You wouldn't dare."

"Oh, wouldn't I?" challenged Mary.

"I'll have them drag you back in," declared Colin smugly.

"Fine, Mr. Rajah," said Mary. "Then I'll just clench my teeth and never tell you one thing. Not even about seeing your father."

"My father?" Colin scooted to the edge of his bed. "Tell me!" he demanded.

Mary pursed her lips.

"He didn't come to see me," Colin said. He slumped back on the bed. "I'll die because he doesn't like me."

"He likes *me*," taunted Mary.

"But hc's *my* father," said Colin.

"Maybe if you weren't always so rude," Mary suggested. "You're so sour you won't even open your windows and let the sun shine into your room."

"How can I?" Colin pouted. "It's raining."

"Even if it weren't raining," said Mary.

"If it weren't raining," Colin said thoughtfully, "maybe I would."

Outside the windows, the rain pounded harder than before.

The rain did not stop that night. Nor the next.

Nor the night after that. One day later in the week, Martha heated a bath for Mary. She poured a pitcher of water directly over Mary's head. Mary looked out the window. The window was as wet as she was.

"Will it ever stop?" she asked.

"Sometimes it rains for a week," said Martha.

"It's been almost a week," Mary sighed.

Martha unfolded a bath towel and held it out to Mary. Mary stepped out of the tub.

"What happens to the plants when it rains this hard?" Mary asked. "Don't they get drowned?" She was worried about her garden.

"Two years ago," said Martha, "everything was wiped out in the storms."

"Everything?" Mary asked.

Martha nodded.

After she was dried and dressed, Mary slipped away from Martha and ran out of the house. She had to get to her garden before everything was ruined! By the time she reached the garden door, she was soaked and shivering. Mary opened the door. It was worse than she had imagined.

The garden was completely flooded. Mary knelt in the mud of the flower bed. The little seedlings that had just begun to grow were floating in big puddles. The new little shoots that had been green and hopeful were now soggy and caked with mud. Worst of all, the Empress of India lily was nearly

washed away. The once proud stalk was shredded and beaten down.

All around the flower bed, the trees drooped from the weight of the rain that soaked their leaves. It looked as if the trees were crying. Mary looked up. Dickon was coming in the garden door.

"Look!" she cried. "It's all ruined! Everything's been killed! The whole thing's dead."

She clawed at the earth and pulled out the bulb. It was so wet and soggy that it fell apart at her touch.

"Even my lily," she cried. She hurled the bulb at Dickon. "You lied to me!" she said. "You told me the rain would be good for the plants!"

Mary collapsed down in the mud. She was sobbing. She slapped angrily at the puddles. Dickon walked toward her and touched her wet hair.

"It's okay," he said softly. "It's not ruined. More flowers will grow to take their place."

"Don't lie," sobbed Mary. Tears were streaming down her face.

"But that's what flowers do," explained Dickon.

"How can I believe you?" Mary sniffed.

"You just can," Dickon shrugged. "That's all."

Dickon put his arm around Mary. She pressed her face against him and cried harder still.

The little girl who had not cried for quite a long time was crying now. She was in a friend's arms. She was safe.

13

That night, finally, the rain began to clear. The next morning, the sun poked through the clouds. It warmed the earth and dried the rain. The smell of spring was in the air.

One bright morning, the sun woke Mary up early. Mary leapt out of bed. She and Dickon had a plan.

Mary peered out her window. She was watching for Mrs. Medlock to leave. Finally, Mrs. Medlock stepped out of the kitchen and got in the carriage. Her shopping basket was slung over her arm. Now was the time! Mary ran to Colin's bedroom.

Mary wasn't the only one waiting for Mrs. Medlock to leave. Dickon was outside the cottage by the front gate. He opened the gate as the carriage rumbled up and latched the gate when it passed. Then he jumped on his pony and galloped off toward the manor house. He had a coil of heavy rope slung over his shoulder.

Inside Colin's bedroom, Mary wheeled Colin up to the windows. The shutters on the windows began to creak and groan. Someone was pulling them open! It was Dickon and the pony outside!

"It's working!" Mary cried excitedly.

Suddenly, the first shutter pulled free of its nails and went clattering down into the yard. Light flooded into the room.

Mary ran to the window. "Keep pulling, Dickon!" she called.

One by one, the shutters pulled free. Colin covered his eyes. He wasn't used to seeing the light. Mary wheeled Colin toward the open window.

"Do you feel it, Colin? Do you?" she asked.

Down in the yard, Dickon was waving to Mary, beckoning her to come down. Mary tore out the door to join him.

"Mary!" Colin called after her. "What about the spores? Can you see them?"

When Mary didn't answer, Colin took his hands from his eyes. The light frightened him. He heard Mary giggling outside. When Colin looked out the window, he saw Dickon on the pony. Dickon was reaching down to pull Mary up with him. Mary hopped up and wrapped her arms around Dickon's waist.

"MARY!" Colin screamed at the top of his lungs. He wanted Mary playing with *him*. Colin screamed louder and kicked his legs. It sounded as if someone were killing him. Martha heard Colin screaming and came running into the room.

"Calm yourself," she said. "Calm yourself, Master Colin."

Martha carried her young master kicking and screaming back to bed. Just then Mary stormed into the house. She was angry that Colin was throwing such a tantrum.

"Miss Mary!" cried Martha. She ran out into the hallway and tried to block Mary's way. "Don't go in there! He's having a dreadful fit. Lord knows what he'll do."

Colin's wails grew louder and louder.

"I don't care!" said Mary. "He's spoiled. Somebody's got to make him stop!"

Mary marched past Martha and into Colin's room. She shouted over the sound of his wails.

"Stop it!" she yelled. "I hate you! You're the most selfish boy who ever was!"

Colin stopped mid-wail. How dare Mary talk to him this way?

"I'm not selfish!" he shouted back at her. "I'm not as selfish as you are! I'm always ill!"

Mary tossed her hair. "Nobody ill could scream like that!" she said.

"I'm going to die!" said Colin.

"What do you know about dying?" Mary shot back. "In India I saw hundreds of people dead."

The two strong-willed children shouted back and forth at each other. Martha stood out in the hall, wringing her hands. She didn't know how to stop them.

Just then, Mrs. Medlock returned from her shopping trip. She heard the shouts all the way from the front hall.

"My *mother* died!" Colin was yelling.

"*Both* my parents died!" Mary shouted back at him.

"I felt a lump on my back," Colin said. "I'll get a hump like my father."

"Where?" asked Mary. She pulled Colin's shirt up and poked at his back. "There's nothing but your bones sticking out," she jeered. "It's because you're so skinny."

Just at that moment, Mrs. Medlock ran in. She could not believe the scene that met her eyes. Colin was sitting in the draft, exposed to the air! And there was Mary, in Colin's room! She was poking at the sick boy's back!

"Get away from him, you beastly girl!" Mrs. Medlock shouted. "You'll kill him!"

14

Mrs. Medlock lunged at Mary, but Mary scrambled behind the pillows, out of reach. Colin flailed his arms to shield his cousin. He was on Mary's side now.

Martha looked on from the edge of the bed. Her lips twitched into a smile. She'd never seen these children so full of life!

"Martha!" Mary shouted excitedly. "Colin doesn't have a lump! Not a one!"

Mrs. Medlock turned on Martha. "You let this wretched child in here?" she cried.

"No, ma'am," stammered Martha. "I didn't."

Mrs. Medlock slapped Martha hard across the face.

"You disobeyed me!" she shouted. "You're fired!"

Martha touched her smarting cheek. She stared

at Mrs. Medlock and ran out of the room. Now it was Colin's turn to yell.

"Mrs. Medlock," he said, pulling himself up to his full, young height. "If you dare even think of letting Martha go, I'll send *you* away!"

Mrs. Medlock stared at him in disbelief.

"Get out of here," Colin ordered her. "I want to be alone with my cousin."

"I beg your pardon?" said Mrs. Medlock.

Colin's young voice boomed through the room. "I'm ordering you to leave!" he said.

Mrs. Medlock did not know what to do. Her eyes darted nervously around the room. She noticed the broken shutters at the windows.

"What on earth has been going on in here?" she asked.

She ran to pull the heavy drapes back across the windows.

"GO!" Colin shouted even louder.

Mrs. Medlock backed toward the door. "I shall," she said. "If only to prevent you from doing harm to yourself with this hysterical shrieking."

When she was gone, Colin turned to Mary and broke into a smile.

"I'm not ill," he said in amazement. "Do you think I could go outside, spores and all?"

Mary giggled. "I don't know anything about spores," she said.

"If we went out," Colin proposed, "we could find the door to my mother's garden."

Mary bit her lip.

"If we found the door," Colin continued, "we could go inside."

Mary didn't know what to say.

"What is it?" Colin asked her.

Mary sighed. "I didn't dare tell you," she said. "I didn't dare because I was so afraid I couldn't trust you."

"What?" Colin asked.

"I've been in the garden," Mary admitted. "I found the key. Weeks ago."

Mary was afraid that Colin would be angry, but he wasn't.

"Tell me," he urged her excitedly.

"When you open the door," she started, "you can't see anything. Then you walk down some stone steps. At the bottom, you realize that you're right in the middle of the ruins of an old church. Did you know there used to be a church here?"

Colin shook his head.

"It must have been in ruins for a long time," said Mary. "Most of it has fallen down. Plants and grass are growing everywhere, all over it."

Colin closed his eyes. He tried to picture the wild, beautiful garden.

"Dickon was right," Mary said softly. "He said

spring would start over again after the rains. And it has."

Colin laid his head in Mary's lap. Mary sang him a lullaby. It was a song her Ayah used to sing her.

As Mary sang, Colin drifted off to sleep. He dreamed about the garden. Roses were everywhere. Crocuses clustered in the bright green grass. A baby robin poked its head out of a speckled blue egg.

Colin also dreamed that his mother was in the garden. She was swinging on the garden swing. Her belly was swollen, as it had been when she was pregnant with him. Colin's mother looked as full of life as the garden she had loved. Light glowed all around.

15

Just as Colin had dreamed, spring did come to the garden. But spring was not the only miracle at Misselthwaite Manor.

One morning, the staff gathered at the foot of the grand staircase in the front hall. Mrs. Medlock was there. So were Martha and the kitchen staff. All of the gardeners were there except Ben Weatherstaff.

Suddenly, everyone looked up. The footman was at the top of the stairs, carrying Colin down. He sat Colin in a wicker wheelchair at the foot of the steps. The little invalid was going to go outside!

Mrs. Medlock bustled over and covered Colin's legs with a blanket. Colin cleared his throat. Everyone was staring at him.

"I am going out in my chair," he announced. "If the fresh air agrees with me, I may go out every day."

Mrs. Medlock wrung her hands.

"When I go," Colin instructed, "no one is to be anywhere about. None of the staff. Not a single gardener. Is that clear?"

Mary was standing next to Colin's chair. She nudged Dickon and tried not to smile.

"Everyone must keep away," Colin instructed firmly, "until I return to the house and send word that they may go back to their work."

"Very good, sir," said the head gardener.

Colin waved his hand to dismiss the staff. Dickon stepped behind the chair and wheeled Colin to the door. Mary followed, as if in a parade. Mrs. Medlock watched anxiously as the children left the house and walked toward the gardens.

Dickon and Mary wheeled Colin through the maze of gardens. When they were out of sight of the house, Dickon pushed the wheelchair faster. The staff knew that the children were going to the garden, but they didn't know that it was the *forbidden* garden. The three children wanted to get safely inside before they were seen.

"Faster!" Colin urged them.

At last they came to the door of the secret garden. Mary unlocked the door and drew an excited breath.

"Here we go," she said.

Colin closed his eyes. He wanted to be surprised.

Dickon and Mary carried Colin and the wheel-chair down the garden steps. The wheelchair was heavy and the ride was bumpy.

"I wish I could help," said Colin. He kept his eyes covered with his hands.

"Don't worry," said Dickon. "Us'll have you walkin' along with us before you know it."

"Me? Walk?" said Colin. He had never thought he might actually *walk*. "Do you think I could?"

"You have legs just like everybody else," Dickon reasoned.

The wheelchair bumped down the last few steps. Dickon wheeled the chair to the edge of the pond.

"Now," said Mary.

Colin took his hands from his eyes and blinked at the bright colors all around him. The garden was in full bloom. Flowers were everywhere.

"Yes," Colin said slowly. "I imagined this."

A light breeze rippled the water in the pond. For a moment, it looked as if the outline of a woman was reflected there. It looked like Colin's mother. Perhaps she was there to welcome her son.

Mary lifted the blanket from Colin's knees. She laid it down on the ground and the three children sat down.

"I'm going to come here tomorrow," Colin said happily, "and the day after, and the day after that." He couldn't remember ever feeling so alive.

Mary ran a rose petal over Colin's cheek.

"Like velvet, isn't it?" she asked.

It seemed that nothing could disturb their perfect afternoon.

Just then, the robin flew overhead. Colin watched the bird fly toward the far wall of the garden. But the robin wasn't the only one Colin saw. He saw a man. The man had climbed up a ladder and was peering over the wall. He was staring at the three children in the garden.

"Who is that man?" asked Colin.

It was Ben Weatherstaff, angry and shaking his fist.

16

Ben Weatherstaff was glaring at Mary. "You miserable little heathen!" he shouted. "I couldn't bear you the first time I laid eyes on you!"

Mary marched up to the wall. Ben Weatherstaff rattled on.

"I never could figure out how you got on my good side," he said. "It must've been that fool robin!"

"It was the robin who showed me the door!" Mary retorted.

Dickon was helping Colin back into his chair. He wheeled Colin up to the wall.

"Do you know who I am?" Colin asked. He sat as tall in his chair as he could.

Ben Weatherstaff blinked. He couldn't believe his eyes. He'd never actually seen Colin, but he knew right away who the boy was.

"You're the little cripple," Ben said. His voice was shaking.

"I'm not a cripple!" Colin shouted angrily. "Who said I'm a cripple? I'm not! I'm not!"

Colin grasped the arms of his wheelchair. With the little strength he had in his arms, he started to push himself up.

Mary sucked in her breath. "You can do it! You can! You can!" she chanted.

Colin planted his weight on his thin, spindly legs. His legs wobbled, but he did not fall down.

"Look at me!" he said proudly. "Just look!"

"You did it!" Mary gasped.

Colin lowered himself back into his chair. Ben Weatherstaff stared. He never thought he would see this boy who'd grown up in a sick bed. He certainly never thought he'd see the boy stand. Ben Weatherstaff wiped an unexpected tear from his cheeks.

"We didn't want you," Colin said to the gardener, "but now you're here. Don't say a word about any of this to anyone. I'll send for you to help us sometimes, but you must come when no one can see you."

Ben Weatherstaff smiled. He had a secret of his own.

"I come here before when no one saw me," he told the children.

"How?" asked Colin. "Nobody's been inside for ten years."

"I come over the wall," explained Ben. "Like I was doing today. The poor roses would've died otherwise. Your mother was so fond of this garden."

Ben Weatherstaff had known his mother! Colin wanted to hear more.

"She used to ask me to look after her roses," Ben explained proudly. "She wouldn't ask anybody else. When she — " Ben choked at the memory of the pretty young woman. "When she . . . went away," he said, "the orders were that no one was to come here. But I come anyway. She gave her orders first."

"I'm glad you did," said Colin. "You'll know how to keep a secret. Come inside. Be quick!"

Ben climbed down from the wall to join the children in the garden. Now, four people were friends in the garden. The secret garden seemed to work its magic on everyone. Children and crotchety old gardeners alike.

As the days wore on, the children came back every chance they could. One morning, Dickon brought a little lamb with him. He'd found the lamb on the moor. It had lost its mother. When Dickon found it, it was hungry and bleating.

Dickon brought the lamb to the garden and fed it milk from a baby bottle. The little lamb drank the milk down hungrily. When the lamb had finished feeding, Dickon lifted it up and stood it on its spindly legs.

"Off you go now," said Dickon.

The lamb tottered away unsteadily. Its legs were shaky, but it walked nonetheless.

Colin watched the little animal. The lamb's shaky legs reminded him of his own. If the lamb was able to walk . . .

Colin struggled to get to his own feet.

"Give me a hand, Dickon," he said.

Dickon grabbed his arm and helped Colin stand. Mary jumped to her feet to watch. When Colin had his balance, Dickon let go.

"You can do it, you can do it," Mary said under her breath.

Colin took a small step. Then another. He was walking! Mary held out her arms. Slowly, one step at a time, Colin walked toward Mary and into her open arms.

17

Colin's legs grew stronger and stronger. Whenever the children went to the garden, he would stand and walk. One night, late, Colin appeared in Mary's doorway.

"Who is it?" Mary whispered, frightened. "Are you a ghost?"

"No, Mary!" Colin answered. "It's me!"

Mary squealed with delight.

"Shh!" Colin quieted her. "Medlock might hear you."

"She'd drop dead if she saw you walking," Mary giggled.

Colin tottered into the room and climbed up onto Mary's bed.

"This is just how I want it to be with my father," he said. "I want to surprise him just like this. I'll walk into his room and say, 'It's me, Father. I'm here.'"

"But he's not due back for a long time," said Mary.

"I want him to see me walk before anyone else does," Colin said fervently. "If only we knew how to find him."

Mary tried to think. There must be a way. Medlock would know how to find Lord Craven, but she'd never tell. Suddenly, Mary remembered something.

"I saw a desk in your father's room," she said, "when I visited him that time. The desk had a lot of papers on it. Maybe one has his address."

She scrambled out of bed.

"Wait here," she told Colin.

Mary slipped soundlessly through the dark halls and into Lord Craven's study. The desk was heaped high with papers, just as she had remembered.

Mary riffled through the papers. She couldn't find Lord Craven's address, but she found something else. It was a stack of photographs, the ones her uncle had stared at that day.

The photographs were of her Aunt Lilias. She was pregnant, sitting on the garden swing. In one photograph, she was leaning over to kiss Lord Craven. Both of them looked very much in love.

Mary took the photographs back to show Colin. Colin stared wistfully at the image of his mother and father. He curled up against Mary for comfort. He wished his father looked that happy now. He wished his father would smile at him.

Just before dawn, Colin crept back to his own room. Mary watched him from the hall.

"What are you doing?" said a voice. It was Mrs. Medlock. She had seen Mary, but luckily she hadn't seen Colin.

"Nothing," Mary said quickly. She scooted back into her own room and shut the door.

That day, when they went to the garden, Colin sat in the garden swing.

"How could she have fallen off?" he asked Mary.

"I don't know," she said.

Colin brushed off the old camera, the one Mary had found her first day in the garden. He set it on its tripod. Mary and Dickon scrambled to the swing to pose. Colin clicked the broken camera as if he were taking photographs of them.

Mary leaned over to tickle Dickon. She threw her legs over his lap. Dickon wrestled with her playfully, and the two children tumbled off the swing and onto the ground.

"Hey!" cried Colin.

Mary and Dickon were laughing. Dickon looked at Mary. He brushed her loose hair from her face. Colin was jealous. Mary and Dickon were having fun without him.

"No!" he shouted at Dickon. He flung the camera

down. "You terrible common boy! Get out of my garden this instant!"

Dickon looked up, stung and surprised. He scrambled to his feet and ran out of the garden.

"Look what you've done!" Mary shouted at Colin. "*You're* the terrible boy! How could you treat him like that?"

Colin knew it was true. He ran after Dickon.

"Dickon, don't go!" he called after his friend. "I'm sorry."

Dickon stopped running and faced Colin squarely. "I know I'm rough from th' moor, but I'm no' your servant," he said. "I'm your friend."

"Yes," said Colin quietly. "You are my friend."

He took Dickon's hand and pulled him back to the garden. Colin was new at having friends.

But he was learning.

18

Though Colin grew stronger each day, Mrs. Medlock didn't suspect. She continued to give him medical treatments. Colin didn't like the fuss at all.

"Stop all this," he said.

Mrs. Medlock had wrapped Colin in hot towels and was filling the tub up with cold water and ice.

"I'm well," Colin protested. "Why won't you write my father and tell him to come back?"

"Because I don't believe you're well at all," said Mrs. Medlock. "Despite what you and your cousin may think, you are still under my care. Your father trusts me to do what's best for you, and that is precisely what I intend to do."

Mrs. Medlock unwrapped the hot towels from Colin's legs. Colin's legs looked stronger. Mrs. Medlock thought they looked sick.

"Look at your legs!" she cried. "They're swollen and red! I knew you had a fever!"

She dumped Colin into the tub.

"If I'm so sick," said Colin, "you ought to send for my father."

Mrs. Medlock lifted Colin from the bath and carried him back to his bed.

"Give me my father's address!" Colin cried, desperately. "I'll write him myself!"

Mrs. Medlock shook her head. She was still convinced Colin was sick. "Heaven knows what's happened," she muttered. "Between that wicked girl and the dangers of the open air. They probably turned over your chair."

Mrs. Medlock pulled up Colin's covers.

"You are to stay in bed," she ordered. "You are not to go into the gardens."

Colin kicked at the covers and screamed. Mrs. Medlock walked out the door. In the hallway she met Mary.

"I'm keeping you children apart," she said. "Colin's a very ill little boy. I've worked too hard and too long to keep him alive to have him killed by a pigheaded, meddlesome little girl!"

Mrs. Medlock pushed Mary into her bedroom and locked the door behind her. Mary waited until she heard Mrs. Medlock leave. Then she headed straight for the tiny little door in the far wall of her room. She went to fetch Colin. They had to meet Dickon in the garden.

Mary and Colin were meeting Dickon because Colin had a plan. He wanted to get his father back. The garden was the perfect place for his plan. The garden seemed to be magical.

The three children waited in the garden until dark fell. When he was finished with his day's work, Ben Weatherstaff joined them. Ben built a large bonfire in a clearing of the garden. Colin ran around the bonfire while Mary danced.

"What would you have me do now, Master Colin?" asked Ben.

"This is an experiment," Colin explained to him. "We're going to make magic. We'll start the chanting in a moment."

"I canna' do no chantin', sir," said Ben. "They turned me out o' th' church choir th' only time I tried it."

Colin pulled Ben into the circle. "Your voice is important," he said. Then Colin started chanting. At first he chanted nonsense words, sounds.

"Heyago ya hoy! Heyada!"

Mary, Dickon, and Ben joined in, repeating the sounds after Colin. As they chanted, the wind started to gust and blow.

Then Colin changed the sounds to words. *"Oh,*

great magic!" he called. "*Please come to me. Send my father here. Don't hide him from me.*"

At that moment, Lord Craven was far away, in a hotel. He was in an armchair, napping. When Colin and the others started chanting, he fell into a dream. In the dream, his wife Lilias was kneeling in the garden. She was young and alive and pretty.

"Archie!" she called to Lord Craven. "Archie!" Her voice was sweet and clear.

"Where are you?" murmured Lord Craven. "Lilias, where are you?"

"In the garden," his wife called out. "Come to the garden!"

Lord Craven awoke.

"I must go!" he said. "I must go tonight! I must get back to Misselthwaite!"

Lord Craven rushed off to pack his bags.

Colin's magic had worked after all.

19

Lord Craven arrived at Misselthwaite the very next day. His carriage pulled up to the little stone cottage outside the front gate. He called to Dickon's mother, who was working there.

"Perhaps you can tell me," he said. "Is there any news of my son?"

Dickon's mother didn't know how much she should reveal.

"My Martha's a maid at the house, sir," she answered. "She's said there have been changes."

Lord Craven put his head in his hands. He was sure something terrible had happened.

The carriage rode past the gate and headed toward the manor house. Inside the house, Martha heard the rumble of the carriage drawing near.

"Mrs. Medlock!" she called. "Mrs. Medlock! There's a carriage coming up the drive!"

No one in the house had expected Lord Craven.

The servants scurried about, preparing for their master's arrival. Mrs. Medlock ran to greet Lord Craven at the door. He pushed right past her.

"Where's my son?" he asked anxiously.

"In his room, my lord, of course," said Mrs. Medlock.

Lord Craven started up the stairs. Mrs. Medlock hurried after him.

Lord Craven marched to Colin's bedroom. He threw open the door. Colin's bed was empty. The broken shutters banged loudly at the open windows.

"Where's my son?" Lord Craven demanded.

Mrs. Medlock ran to the bed and pulled back the covers, as if Colin might be hiding.

"Here. He should be here," she stammered.

Lord Craven saw the portrait of his wife. The curtain was drawn back and Lilias looked out at him, no longer hidden.

"What's happened?" he asked.

"It's that child Mary, my lord," Mrs. Medlock complained. "She's created absolute havoc here. I can't control her."

Lord Craven headed for Mary's room.

"Mary must be sent away," Mrs. Medlock said, as she chased down the hall after Lord Craven. "She'll kill Colin for sure. She has no regard for the fragile state of his health and does exactly as she pleases."

Lord Craven arrived at Mary's door. Mrs. Medlock's key guarded the lock.

"You lock her in?" he asked Mrs. Medlock.

"I've had to," Mrs. Medlock said, defending herself. "That's how wild she is."

Lord Craven turned the key and threw open the door. The room was empty, just as Colin's had been.

"I beg your pardon, my lord," said a voice behind them. It was Martha. "But perhaps they're in the garden."

"I don't see how, sir," Mrs. Medlock cut in. "That's quite impossible."

Lord Craven stalked back down the hall. Mrs. Medlock stumbled after him. She was nearly crying.

"I've done my best, sir," she said. "I have. But with that child defying me at every turn . . ."

"She's a *child*, Medlock," Lord Craven said crossly. "Just a child. I left *you* in charge."

When they reached the steps of the manor, Lord Craven wheeled around to face Mrs. Medlock.

"You stay here," he barked at her.

Lord Craven hurried down the walk, toward the garden. He did not know what he would find. Mrs. Medlock collapsed on the steps. She buried her face in her hands. Martha stepped out and stroked Mrs. Medlock's hair to comfort her. Mrs. Medlock cried and cried.

20

As Lord Craven drew near the secret garden, he heard sounds of laughter. At the door to the garden, the ivy was loose and swinging free. Lord Craven pulled back the curtain of ivy and tried the door. It was open. Lord Craven stopped at what he saw.

In the garden, Mary and Dickon were blindfolding Colin. They were playing "Blind Man's Bluff." They spun Colin around.

"Now come and get us!" Mary called.

Mary giggled and ducked into the bushes. Dickon ducked in behind her. None of the three children had seen Lord Craven come in the garden door.

Colin took a careful step forward. He waved his arms, looking for his friends. Lord Craven started down the garden stairs. He stared at his son in disbelief. The last time he had seen Colin, Colin had been in bed, unable to walk. Now he was outside, in the garden, on his feet and laughing with friends.

Mary peeked out from her hiding place. She saw Lord Craven standing in front of Colin. Mary nudged Dickon to look, too.

As Mary and Dickon watched, Colin stumbled forward, waving his arms. He edged up to his father. His hand grazed his father's chest. Colin knew he had bumped into somebody, but he was still blindfolded. He touched his father's cloak. He touched his father's face. Could it be? He pulled down the blindfold. It was! It was his father!

"I can't believe it," Lord Craven whispered. His voice was choked with tears.

"You're here!" said Colin. "The magic worked!"

"But the last time I saw you — " Lord Craven started to say.

The last time he had seen Colin, Colin had been a pale, sickly invalid. Now his son was strong and healthy. Lord Craven had not even thought it possible.

Lord Craven put his arms around Colin and hugged him tightly. Mary and Dickon stepped out from their hiding place. Lord Craven looked at the garden all around him. It was tended and cared for. Everything was in bloom.

"The garden!" he said in amazement.

"Let me show you," said Colin. "Come on."

Colin pulled his father down the garden path.

Mary was glad to see Colin and his father so happy, but she was sad herself. She wished she had a father who would return and hug her tightly. Her father was dead. So was her mother.

Mary thought Lord Craven hadn't even noticed her when he'd looked around the garden. She thought she wasn't wanted. She slipped out the garden door. She wanted to be alone. She headed for the moor.

On the moor, the wind whipped and howled. Mary's eyes stung with tears. If she wasn't wanted at Misselthwaite, she didn't know where she would go.

Suddenly, above the wind, Mary heard her name. Someone was calling her.

"Mary!" came the cry. "Ma-a-ary!"

Mary turned around. It was Lord Craven calling. He was walking toward her on the moor. His dark cape whipped in the wind.

"Mary," he said. "Why are you out here by yourself?"

Sobs welled up in Mary. She could barely talk.

"You're Colin's father," she managed to say. "He wanted you to come back. I'm glad for him that you're here."

Lord Craven studied the sad little girl.

"Didn't *you* want me to come back, too?" he asked.

Tears streamed down Mary's cheeks. Lord Craven put his arms around her and hugged her as he'd hugged his son.

"Come back inside, Mary," he said softly.

It seemed someone loved Mary after all.

Lord Craven took Mary's hand and led her back to the secret garden. The robin flew above them, chirping happily.

Inside the garden, a light, airy figure smiled at the reunion. It was the spirit of Lilias. Her son was now healthy. Her husband had returned. Her niece had a home. And it had all happened inside her own beautiful garden.

Though no one seemed to notice, the spirit of Lilias passed from the garden and headed out toward the moor. She could leave her family now. Everything she had hoped for them had at last come true.